Past Eight O'Clock

Past Eight O'Clock

Goodnight Stories

Joan Aiken

Pictures by

Jan Pieńkowski

VIKING KESTREL

also by Joan Aiken and Jan Pieńkowski

A Necklace of Raindrops
The Kingdom Under the Sea
Tale of a One-way Street

VIKING KESTREL

Viking Penguin Inc., 40 West 23rd Street, New York, New York 10010, U.S.A.

First published in Great Britain by Jonathan Cape Ltd, London, 1986

First American Edition Published in 1987

Text copyright © Joan Aiken Enterprises Ltd, 1986
Illustrations copyright © Jan Pieńkowski, 1986
All rights reserved

Printed in Great Britain by Scotprint Ltd, Edinburgh

1 2 3 4 5 90 89 88 87

Contents

From Joan
to my granddaughter Arabel
From Jan to Luki

Past Eight O'Clock

enny and her grandmother, old Mrs Heron, lived in the very small town of Troy-on-the-Water. Jenny was seven, her grandmother was seventy-seven. Where were Jenny's father and mother? Her father was a sea captain, sailing at sea on his ship; her mother had died three years before.

Granny Heron had a cheerful nature, white hair done in a knob on top, a black dress, and a blue and white apron.

Jenny and her grandmother got on very well. They played lots of conversation games. For instance, they had a pretend cat, called Gladiolus, and they used to argue about him.

"Gladiolus is sitting on my lap," Granny Heron used to say, knitting away at a sock for Jenny. "He's purring, and being ever so good, not playing with the wool, though he'd like to."

"*No*, Granny! You're quite *wrong*! Gladiolus is on *my* lap! And I'm scratching under his chin."

"Well you'd better take him out in the garden for an airing, child."

They both knew what Gladiolus looked like: he was a tortoiseshell tom, black and white and orange, with green eyes, black ears, and white whiskers. And he was bigger than any common cat.

Sometimes Jenny used to say, "Why can't we have *two* pretend cats, Granny? Then we'd have a cat for each of our laps."

"No, no, we couldn't possibly afford two pretend cats," Granny Heron always said. *"One* is trouble enough."

Jenny had a school friend, a boy called Erl, who lived next door and always walked home from school with her. Jenny helped Erl with his sums, because she enjoyed adding and dividing and multiplying, while Erl couldn't see the sense of it; and Erl helped Jenny when they played games outside. He was marvellously clever at catching balls, could make a ball come right into his hand, from the other side of the playground, like a bird into its nest. Or, he could make it turn in its course, and drop into Jenny's hand. He was a useful friend, and very kind-hearted.

In Troy, the town where they lived, there was a law that all children under fourteen must be in bed by eight o'clock at night. If children were found out of bed after that time, their parents had to pay a hundred pounds to the town council; if they had not *got* a hundred pounds, they had to work for six months at cleaning the town drains. And any child caught out of bed at night was forbidden to watch television for six months.

What a strange law! you will think. The reason for it was that, long, long ago, there had been huge flocks of dragons in that part of the country, who used to fly round and snap up children at night. Now all the dragons were gone and forgotten; but still the law remained, and nobody was allowed to break it: children must be in bed by eight.

To make sure that the law was properly kept, a Child Warden walked around the streets of Troy all night. He peered through windows, he stared down dark alleys, he scanned the playgrounds with his powerful torch, he groped under the arches of the Butter Cross, he poked with a stick under bridges, searched in people's back yards, listened outside the entrances of clubs and churches; and every night he rang dozens of doorbells and insisted on going into people's houses, looked into their parlours, kitchens, playrooms, and dining rooms, to make sure that no children were illegally staying up to watch TV or listen to records, or do their school work, or just talk to their parents.

After eight, any bang on the knocker or ring at the doorbell would send children racing up the stairs, tearing off their clothes, and hurling themselves into bed, often without washing or even brushing their teeth. A hundred-pound fine, or having to work in the drains, was bad enough – but six months without TV was *horrible*!

10

Just the same, it often happened; people were always being caught; and the drains of Troy-on-the-Water were the cleanest in the land.

Most people thought the law was silly, and should be done away with; and *everybody* hated the Child Warden. He was a spiteful old man called Bill Winks; but people spoke of him as Weevilly or Weaselly Winkie, because of the wee-villy, weaselly way in which he crept and sidled about the streets. He wore soft-soled sneaker shoes, and an aged black felt cloak with a hood, which covered him from head to foot, so that it was not easy to spot him in the shadows as he peered under cars or between the cracks of curtains.

Weaselly Winkie was hardly ever seen when it was light; all day he slept on the sofa in his nasty, damp, dirty, little cottage by the gasworks, so that he would be able to walk about the town all night.

If he ever *did* pay a hasty visit to the super-market, to buy cereal and jelly, which was all he ever ate, or batteries for his torch, the children used to collect together and follow him, teasingly singing:

"Weavilly Winkie runs through the town
Like a black spider in his black gown,
Rapping at the front door, crying through the lock
Are the children all in bed, it's past eight o'clock?

"Hoo-ha-hoo! Hoo-ha-ha!
Weeeee-eeee-villy Winkie!"

Sometimes they used to shout "Old tenpenny!" because he was paid ten pence by the council for every child he caught out of bed.

Some people thought he was a retired witch; or a witch who had gone out of business because people had no use for him. Everyone agreed that he was a mean, nasty old man, who liked to cause trouble and unhappiness if he could, and that he was just right for his unpleasant job.

Weaselly Winkie had a special grudge against Jenny's friend Erl. Why? Who can say? Perhaps it was because Erl had bright red hair and bright blue eyes, and a loud voice and a lively tongue. Erl's voice was always among the loudest when they sang:

"Hoo-ha-hoo! Hoo-ha-hoo!
Sneaky old Winkie, banging at the lock,
Are the kids in beddybyes, it's past eight o'clock?
Weeee-eeeee-selly Winkie!"

Erl, who was afraid of nothing and nobody, had once crept up close to Winkie's tumbledown

12

cottage and looked through his window.

"Why shouldn't I? He looks through *our* windows often enough! He has a huge glass barrel in his pantry, and it's almost full of tenpenny pieces!"

"That's his savings from all the children he's caught," said Jenny's granny.

"Perhaps when it's quite full he'll retire," said Jenny hopefully. She hated the Child Warden's sharp little black eyes and sour creased face and spiteful ways.

"And when he's not asleep," said Erl, "he sits at a greasy old round table, playing clock patience with a greasy old pack of cards."

"I wish he played cards at night too," said Jenny, "instead of bothering us."

One snowy winter afternoon Jenny walked home with Erl rather faster than usual. She was worried about Granny Heron, who had a bad cold. In the morning Granny had been flushed and rather cross, which was not like her at all. She had coughed a lot and not eaten any breakfast. Jenny had begged her to stay in the house all day, but Granny said there was the shopping to do.

"I could do it, Granny!"

"You? There's too many things for your little head to remember – eggs and flour and oranges and fish for Gladiolus."

"But, Granny – " Jenny was beginning to say, "Gladiolus doesn't eat *real* fish – " when her

granny almost pushed her out of the door, saying, "Hurry up now, or you'll be late for school."

So Jenny was worried about her granny. And when she got home she became more worried still. The place was in a muddle, with things half begun and not finished, the fire was out, tea not made, and, worst of all, Granny was lying on the half-made bed, very flushed, with her hair all in a tangle, and muttering to herself, "That cat's been *so* naughty, crying to go out all day. Mind you don't let him out the door, child! Give him a saucer of milk and some of that fish I bought, and tell him to behave himself."

Jenny didn't dare try to argue with her grandmother, for it only made the old lady more feverish and wild. Erl helped her tidy up the bed, and light the fire, then they made a pot of tea and persuaded Granny Heron to swallow a cupful. Then the two children did their homework together, and Jenny helped Erl with his sums. Then he said he had better go home, it was getting close to eight o'clock. Erl's mother kept a little shop next door to the Herons', where she sold candles and string and soap; his father was a soldier in the army, far away.

"If you need me, Jenny, or get anxious, bang on the bedroom wall," said Erl.

The two children could visit each other over the roof, climbing out of the skylight windows of their bedrooms. It was a bit dangerous, in case the

Child Warden spotted them, but just the same they sometimes did it on foggy nights.

After Erl had gone home, Jenny tried to persuade her granny to go to bed.

"*I* have to go up in five minutes, Granny, so *you'd* better go too!"

But old Mrs Heron wouldn't.

"No, no, child, I have to sit up and watch for that naughty cat. Do you know, he's been out *three hours*? He got out, although I tried to stop him." And she went to the front door and opened it, letting in a gust of snowy wind, and called, "Puss, puss, puss, puss, puss!"

"No, Granny, no," said Jenny, almost crying because she was so worried. "Look – Gladiolus is sitting right here by the fire, good as gold!"

"No, he isn't!" snapped the old lady, without even turning round. "Puss, puss, puss, come here! If you think you see him in front of the fire, child, you're *imagining* things!" And she stuck her head out into the snowy street and called, "Gladiolus? Where are you, you wicked cat?"

At that moment the Child Warden walked by Mrs Heron's house, and he looked sharply past

Granny through the open door into the kitchen.

"Better send that child up to bed, Mrs Heron," he said sharply, "She hasn't left herself much time to wash and brush her teeth – it's five minutes to eight now."

Weevilly Winkie didn't like Jenny, because she was Erl's friend.

"I've lost my cat," said old Mrs Heron crossly, taking no notice of what Winkie had said. "My cat Gladiolus is out in the snow."

Now if there was one thing the Child Warden *detested* – besides children – it was cats. They made him sneeze. They brought him out in a rash. If a cat rubbed against his leg, he felt as if he were going to choke. If one sat on his lap he thought he would suffocate. Cats terrified him. He would run fifty metres if he saw a cat in the street, and he kept a catapult to shoot pellets at them.

The children knew this of course, and to tease him they would call,

"Weevilly Winkie, watch out for the cats,
There's two right behind you, a-waiting to scratch!
Mee-yew, mee-yow, Weeeee-villy Winkie!"

So when Granny Heron told him that she was looking for her cat, Winkie thought she was doing it just to annoy him. For he knew perfectly well that she had no cat. He knew all the families in town who had cats.

"You watch your tongue, Missis!" he snarled at her. "You treat me with respect! I'm an official of the town. And you'd better get that child off to bed – I warn you!"

He spoke so fiercely that Granny Heron did go back inside her house and shut the door. And Jenny crept up the stairs to bed. But twenty minutes later she heard a tremendous banging and clattering, coming from downstairs. Jenny got out of bed, looked down the stairs, and saw Granny Heron wandering about the kitchen. She was turning things upside down, pulling out drawers, unfolding all the tidily folded teacloths, and rummaging in the back parts of cupboards.

She was calling, "Puss, puss, puss!"

Jenny ran softly down the stairs.

"Granny, Granny, you *must* come to bed!"

"I can't, I can't come, child, till I've found that naughty cat!"

And Granny went off to the back door, opened that, and called, "Here, pussy, pussy, pussy, pussy, Gladiolus!"

In blew a blast of snow.

Jenny, deeply, deeply worried, ran back upstairs and banged on her bedroom wall. Then she opened the skylight, in spite of the snow that poured in. Very soon, in crept Erl, brushing the

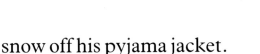

snow off his pyjama jacket.

"Erl, I think Granny's very ill! What should I do?"

Just then Granny herself came up to Jenny's little room. She did not seem at all surprised at the sight of Erl, but said, "Jenny! You will have to get dressed and go out to look for that naughty cat. And you must *not* come back till you find him!"

Jenny looked at Erl, who gave her a tiny nod.

"All right, Granny," said Jenny, sniffing back her tears; and she dressed, and put on her warm coat and hood and boots.

"I'll go with Jenny to help her find the cat," said Erl to old Mrs Heron. "But first I'll fetch my mum to come and sit with you, Missus."

Erl slipped back through the skylight. His mother had just closed her shop; so she agreed to come round and sit with Mrs Heron.

"We're going to go for the doctor, Mum," Erl told her. "Mrs Heron's proper poorly."

"Eh, dear, your going out at this time is a nasty risk. I wish *I* could go, that I do," said Erl's mother. But she could not, for she was very lame, and the doctor's house was way over on the other side of the town. It would have taken her all night to walk there. "Well," she sighed, "mind how you go, and look sharp. I can see you do right to go, for the old lady does seem very middling."

Erl and Jenny slipped out into the snowstorm, looking hard both ways for the Child Warden.

They would have to run like hares if they sighted him, for neither Granny Heron nor Erl's mother could possibly pay a hundred-pound fine. And it was not to be *thought* of that they should work in the town drains for six months.

All went well till the two children were half-way across town, past the Butter Cross where the four main streets met. The snow was falling so thickly – like slices of white bread blowing in the wind – that no sensible person was out. You could hardly see across the street.

"Only another block to go now," panted Erl.

Then – at that moment, like a black bat, the Child Warden sprang from behind a big flat headstone in the churchyard, where he was lurking.

"Aha! – I see *children*! Now I've got you!" he squawked, in his rusty, grating voice, and he came flapping after them, his cloak trailing behind him like one tattered wing.

Erl and Jenny ran as fast as they could – and they were both very fast runners – but Weevilly Winkie was faster still. The snow underfoot was horribly slippery, their feet couldn't grip the ground, and they could hear him coming thump-thump-thump along behind, closer and closer.

"You go on, I've an idea," gasped Erl. He stopped and turned to face the Child Warden, clapping his hands together in a queer way.

Instantly, a whole pack of shiny new cards flew out from between his flat hands – blew out and scattered in a slippery trail, all along the street.

"Those cards are for you, Weevilly!" called Erl. And then he turned and ran for dear life again, after Jenny.

Weaselly Winkie couldn't resist the pack of new cards, all red and blue and black and white and shiny, that lay scattered in a trail on top of the snow. Puffing and grumbling, he stopped to pick them up, and shuffle them and count them and

put them in his pocket. At last he had them all. Erl had hoped he might want to go home and play a game with them. But no, he started after the children once more.

By now they had nearly reached the doctor's house; but just before they got to it, Weaselly Winkie caught up with them once more and grabbed an arm of each.

"Aha! I know *you*!" he said gloatingly to Erl. "And I know *you*!" he said sourly to Jenny. "Well? Have you anything to say for yourselves, before I take you round to the lock-up?"

"Yes!" said Jenny stoutly, though her heart was in her freezing cold gumboots. "I'm out on a fit and proper errand, fetching Dr Widderby for

my granny, who is very poorly. And Erl came to keep me company."

"*That's* no excuse. *That's* no excuse at *all*," said the Child Warden. "I don't need to tell you, Miss, you know perfectly well yourself, that there are only two reasons accepted as fit and proper causes for a child to be out after eight o'clock at night. One of them is to fetch the doctor for a *parent*. But old Mrs Heron is *not* your parent, Miss, she's only your grandmother. So that will be a hundred-pound fine for her, or else she'll have to work for six months in the drains."

"Oh, no, *no*!" said Jenny, gasping with cold and horror and misery. "Oh, *please* don't –"

"And it'll be the same for *your* mother," said

the Child Warden triumphantly to Erl. "And let that be a lesson to you both – "

"Wait – just wait a minute!" said Erl. "You've forgotten the *second* fit and proper reason for a child to be out after eight."

"Doesn't apply!" said Weevilly Winkie sharply, "as there isn't any – "

"Oh, but there is!" said Erl. "The *second* fit and proper reason for a child to be out after eight is if he or she is searching for a lost cat. And as it happens we *are* searching for Mrs Heron's cat Gladiolus, who is lost – "

"But she doesn't *have* a real cat. She doesn't have a – "

"And, what's more – *there he is!*" shouted Erl joyfully. He put his fingers to his lips and blew a long, whistling call. "Here, puss!" he called. "Here, pussy, pussy, pussy, pussy, pussy!" – and through the snow and fog came galloping the largest tortoiseshell cat that Jenny had ever seen, with black and white and ginger patches, with green eyes and black ears and an orange nose and white whiskers.

"Gladiolus!" gasped Jenny, as he sprang on to her shoulder. "Why, it really *is* Gladiolus!"

Weevilly Winkie gasped even louder, at the sight of the enormous cat. He turned a greenish kind of white, and let out a queer, breathless, terrified wail. Then he turned and fled away through the snow, moaning as he went:

"Oh-oh-oh-oh-oh! OH!"

The two children hurried on in the other direction and rang the doctor's doorbell. Luckily he had just got home from another case. He drove Erl and Jenny (still clutching the enormous Gladiolus) back to Mrs Heron's little house.

"You were lucky the Child Warden didn't catch you," he said as he drove.

"He did, but he let us go again," said Erl.

"Because we had the cat," said Jenny, stroking Gladiolus.

The doctor gave Mrs Heron some medicine which soon did her good; but what did her even more good was the sight of the tortoiseshell cat.

"*There* you are at last, Gladiolus!" she said fondly. "Don't you dare stay out so long, ever again!"

When the doctor and Erl and his mother had all left, Gladiolus jumped into Granny's armchair, by the fireplace. And there he slept all night long, and in the morning he was still there. And in the morning Granny was much better.

The Child Warden was never seen again. His little house was empty, the greasy cards still on the table, and the glass barrel full of silver coins in the pantry. As he never came back to claim it, the money was used to buy swings for the children's playground. And, as nobody else wanted the job of Child Warden, the law that said children must be in bed by eight could not be enforced.

So now children in Troy-on-the-Water can stay up all night if they want; and some of them do.

But they still sing:

"Weevilly Winkie, in your black gown
Like a skinny spider, running through the town,
Rapping at the windows, bawling at the lock –
Are the kids all in bed, it's gone eight o'clock!"

Erl and Jenny are still best friends. She still does his sums for him. And he makes balls and birds fly into her hands from all over the playground.

Gladiolus, the magic cat, still lives with Jenny and Mrs Heron. Sometimes he sits on one lap, sometimes on the other.

Your Cradle is Green

O nce upon a time there were two towns, called Mucham and Littleham. In Mucham the people very often had too many children, more than they could feed. While, in Littleham, many people had no children at all. Why was this? Nobody knows.

In between the two towns there stretched a wide, dark wood, with a rocky river winding through the middle of it. And beside this river was an old, old house, all grown over with ivy. Once, long ago, it had been the school where the children of Littleham went to learn their lessons. But now there were not enough children to make it worth having a school. Now the Littleham children went, by bus, to the school in Mucham. As it wasn't needed for a school, the old ivy-covered house had been turned into a Home.

To this Home, the people of Mucham who had more children than they could keep used to bring the ones they couldn't afford, and left them there to be looked after by a girl called Gerda.

Gerda was a very kind person, and she took the best possible care of all the babies who were brought to her. She fed them on bread-and-milk

and honey and wild strawberries, she read aloud to them, she played games with them, she pushed them in the garden swing, or on the rocking-horse, she took them for walks, and sang them to sleep at night. And they all loved her. As soon as Gerda came into the room, all their eyes followed her, wherever she went.

Babies didn't generally stay with Gerda for very long. What nearly always happened was this. A few days after some sad father or mother in Mucham had said, "We can't feed any more children. This last one will have to go," and had carried the small wrapped bundle down through the wood and left it on Gerda's doorstep – a very few days after Gerda had taken in the new one, and washed it and hugged it and fed it and sung it to sleep – some excited person from Littleham would decide that was just the very baby for them. And so it would be carried to a new home, to be named and cherished and hugged and given toys.

So, week by week, the children under Gerda's care came and went; not often were there more than nine or ten, and they seldom stayed more than a few months at the longest.

Gerda never gave the children real names while they stayed with her. It was for their new parents to do that, she thought. So she found for

each baby a cradle-name, a name to be going on with: one would be called Toes, another Strawberry, another Starlight, another Chicory, another Chaffinch, another Goosefeather – depending on what time of day it was when she found them, or what they had with them.

For the real parents, hating to leave their children but not wanting to linger, would mostly put down a baby on the doorstep and then race away into the darkness of the wood, as fast as if all the king's horses were after them. Yet mostly they left some token behind with the child – a nut, a feather, a flower – so that, perhaps, one day, if things had gone better with them, they might come back and say, "I left you a child on St Benjamin's Eve five years ago. He had a piece of bread in his hand. Who took him in?"

Gerda had a special lullaby for each of her

children. For one it would be:

"Hushabye, Strawberry, snug in your cot,
Sleep just a little and dream a lot – "

for another:

"Walk into sleep on your ten pink Toes,
What you'll find there, nobody knows,
Wake in the morning, safe and well,
What you will bring back, who can tell?"

to another:

"Goosefeather baby, close your eyes,
Gerda will sing your lullaby;
Maybe at daybreak a lady will come
With a silken shawl to carry you home."

to another:

"Lullay, my Starlight,
Drowse and hush;
Fall into sleep
Like a bird in a bush."

for another:

"Rockaway, Chicory, rockaway, child,
Rock on the wings of the wind so wild,
Sleep while it roars, wake when it dies,
Morning's the time to open your eyes."

Each of Gerda's children had his or her own special lullaby. And when they left her, she never

used the old songs for newcomers; no, she always made up new ones. And the children, when they left her, never forgot what she had sung to them. However happy they were with their new families (and mostly they were *very* happy, with parents who had longed for them beforehand, and had come to choose them, and loved them specially well) – yet in some closed cupboard of their memories they always kept the sound of Gerda's singing; to the very end of their lives.

But there was *one* among Gerda's babies who stayed with her on and on; who was never chosen and taken away by a new foster parent. This was a little boy who had been left on the doorstep of the orphan home one windy October night. All his clothes and wrappings were dazzling bright green; and the cradle that he lay in was woven out of grass, which had a sweet scent and was also bright, bright green. The boy who lay in it was beautiful, with dark brown eyes and gold-brown hair; he never cried; but he hardly ever smiled, either. He was solemn and thoughtful, but kind and gentle to the other children.

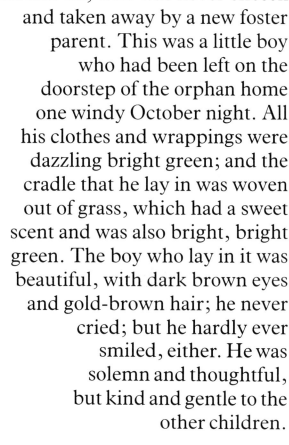

Why did no foster parent ever choose him?
Because he was so small.

When Gerda first took him in, he was *tiny* – smaller than her two fists placed side by side. And during the time that she kept him – though she fed him, like the others, on bread and honey, apples and oranges, lettuce and rhubarb and milk and wild strawberries – he grew very, very slowly, much more slowly than the other children. He ate just as much as the rest, and seemed to thrive; he was active and bright and handsome; but only half the size of the smallest of his companions. Gerda called him Greenboy.

And when she sang him to sleep she sang:

"Hushabye, baby, your cradle is green,
Father's a nobleman, mother's a queen.
Where have they gone? Far, far away –
When will they come? How can I say?"

Greenboy always listened carefully to this song, with his dark brown eyes fixed on Gerda's face.

Some of Gerda's children stayed with her for so short a time that they never learned to talk, or perhaps only a few words, "Gerda" and "swing", "honey", "milk" and "morning".

But Greenboy learned to talk very well. And he learned to draw. Amazing pictures he drew, spinning-wheels that really seemed to spin, flights of stairs that went up and up, horses that seemed to gallop, houses that you could almost walk into, they looked so real.

"Where did you get that idea from, Greenboy?" Gerda or the other children sometimes asked him, and he would mostly answer, "Oh, I dreamed it."

Greenboy learned to count, too. He was clever and nimble at counting, as some children are clever at skipping or somersaulting. First he counted on his fingers and toes; then in the air, then inside his head. He could count in all kinds of ways – two-four-six-eight; or three-six-nine-twelve; or five-ten-fifteen-twenty; or twenty-forty-sixty-eighty-a hundred. Soon he had left all the other children far behind in his counting (*some* of them never learned to count at all); after a while he had left even Gerda behind.

"Where do you expect to get to, with all your counting and counting, Greenboy?" the others asked him.

And Greenboy would answer, "I shan't know till I get there, shall I?"

Sometimes he counted backwards, and put in all the in-between bits, halves and quarters and even smaller parts; sometimes he counted in a circle. When they were all out playing in the grassy garden, he counted leaves; when they played in the brook he counted bubbles.

Greenboy was always very kind to the other children; he helped comfort them when they were first left on Gerda's doorstep, puzzled and hungry and crying for their real mothers and fathers; he hugged them and fed them and taught them games; and then, when they were chosen by new parents, and taken away again, he helped console their sad friends who were left behind.

"It may not be for long. Perhaps you will meet again soon. Perhaps you will be living next door to each other and meet at school," he used to say.

"How do you know so much, Greenboy?" Gerda asked him once.

"By listening to you," he said.

One day Chicory, Greenboy's best friend, was chosen by two foster parents who had come looking for a child, and took a liking to Chicory.

They seemed a pleasant pair. They were called Mr and Mrs Amber, she a round, rosy-faced woman with untidy black hair, he a tall, shabby man with a dreamy look.

"We've always wanted a baby, but we never thought of coming here before," said Mr Amber.

Greenboy approved of the Ambers; he thought his friend Chicory would be happy living with them. But the Ambers' dog was a different matter. Greenboy didn't like him at all. He was a smooth, sharp, brisk, bustling, white terrier, with one brown ear and one white; the dog was called Saxon, and he jumped about and barked and snarled and made little biting snapping dashes at all the children, who squeaked and ran away.

"Saxon won't hurt you, don't worry," said Mr Amber vaguely. "He just isn't used to children, that's all."

Saxon looked as if he did not *mean* to become

used to children. He had a red gleam in his eye, as he snapped at Starlight's ankle and drew blood.

"You will have to keep him out in a kennel while you and Chicory are all getting used to each other," said Gerda firmly, as she put a bandage round Starlight's ankle.

"Oh, Saxon's *never* been in a kennel, he'd not abide it," said Mrs Amber.

"Saxon and the boy (we'll call the boy William, what kind of a name is *Chicory* for a child?) – he and the boy will soon settle down together," said Mr Amber absently. He did not seem at all bothered. "Come along, Annie, let's be getting home. And I thank you kindly, miss."

They walked away, with Chicory between them, looking just a little scared, and Saxon following behind, growling and grumbling to himself, with the red spark still in his eye.

Gerda stared after them with a troubled expression.

But Greenboy sent a noose of numbers speeding after the dog Saxon; one, nine, seventeen, twenty-five, thirty-three, forty-one…

which caught the dog round his neck and swung him into the air and slung him into the brook and filled him with water until he was gulping and choking and soaking and soused and dowsed and quenched and drenched and just as upset as a dog can possibly be.

"Just don't you try *anything* on my friend Chicory – or that will happen to you again, every time!" Greenboy called after the dog, in number language; and Saxon scrambled out of the brook, and flipped his white ear, and flopped his brown ear, and shambled on homewards, puzzled and slipping and dripping and quite subdued.

"Come on children – it's nearly time for tea. But we'll play one game of ring o' roses first," said Gerda, a little sadly.

She hadn't noticed what had happened to Saxon. But she always grieved when one of her children went away, no matter how many new ones might arrive to take its place.

That evening a new baby girl called Holly was found shivering on the doorstep, wrapped in no more than a scrap of towelling – her parents must have been dreadfully poor; and Greenboy helped Gerda warm her and bath her and give her some milk.

"She can have my grass cradle," Greenboy said, "I'm growing too big for it."

This was true. At last he had outgrown it. His feet stuck over the end.

So Holly was put snugly into the grass cradle, and Gerda sang to her:

"Hushabye, Holly, sleep and dream,
Hark to the trees and the sound of the stream;
Fathers and mothers come and go
But the brook in the forest will always flow."

Holly soon stopped crying and fell asleep, clasping her prickly holly leaf.

Then Gerda sang to all the other children, one by one.

"Now it's my turn," said Greenboy, when all the rest were asleep. He looked at Gerda in a strange way, and said, "Am I your special one?"

"You know I don't have a special," said Gerda. "I never have a special."

This was true. She never had favourites. She was as fond of each one as all the others.

But just the same she thought in her heart that perhaps Greenboy *was* her special; because he was so wise, because she thought no foster parents were ever going to take him away. What would become of him?

She sang:

"Hushabye, Greenboy, your cradle is green,
Father's a nobleman, mother's a queen.
Where have they gone to? Far, far away –
When will they seek you? How can I say?"

By the time she had finished singing, it was

dark in the room where the children slept.
Greenboy was lying in a small bed, the one that,
up until today, had been used by Chicory. But it
was so dark, so very dark, that, looking down at
the bed, Gerda could not see him.

"Greenboy?" she said softly. "Are you asleep?"

He did not answer. But she put her hand
down, just to feel his small silky head. Then she
stole away and left the room full of sleeping
children.

In the morning, Greenboy was gone. No one
had heard or seen him go; he had just vanished.

Sometimes, Gerda wondered if he had ever
been there, in the house, at all.

But she did see him once, in a dream, just once. He was standing just across the brook, on the bank, and he smiled at her.

Then he raised his hand, stretched it out, and called softly, "Gerda? Can you hear me, Gerda? If ever – some day – somebody leaves *you* on a doorstep – outside a door – maybe I'll be waiting inside that door to take you in – and then it will be *my* turn to sing you to sleep..."

Pappa's Going to Buy you a Mocking Bird

Once there was a girl called Belinda, but her pappa called her Honeybee. Every night, when he came home from the coalmine, he sang her a goodnight song.

Who looked after Belinda in the daytime? Her granny.

Where was her mum? In hospital. But she would be home soon.

One night, Belinda's pa came home from work. "What was it like in the mine today, Pappa?"

"Dark, my honeybee. Dark and noisy. Things go thump and things go clang. And the coal trundles along on the trolley."

Belinda looked at the coal burning away in the fire, red and bright. She thought about how it would look rolling along on a trolley – like a necklace of red beads.

Then her pa took her on his knee and he sang:

"Hush, my honeybee, don't say a word,
Pappa's going to buy you a mocking bird..."

44

Then off skipped Belinda, upstairs to bed in her cornery little bedroom with its window that looked over the steep valley and away across the river to the other mountain.

She went straight to sleep. And she began to dream. She dreamed that her pappa gave her a beautiful grey and white bird, tame and friendly as a person, that would sit on her shoulder, or perch on the top of her head, and take a cherry or a cake-crumb from her fingers.

But would that bird sing?

Not a note! Not a single note!

"Please, please sing to me, Mocking Bird!" said Belinda.

But the mocking bird shook its head.

Then, with a flip and a waft of its wings, it flew away from Belinda, down the hill, across the brook at the bottom, and up the other side on to the distant mountain.

There sat a boy on a rock, watching. He put out his arm sideways, like a sign-post. And the mocking bird flew up the hill to him and perched on his wrist. Then, far, far away in the distance, Belinda could hear it begin to sing.

Oh, how it sang! It twittered and rippled, it chirruped, it chuckled and cheeped, whistled and fluted, warbled, carolled, lilted, quavered, trilled, and thrilled.

Why should it sing to that boy and not to me? Belinda wondered sadly.

Next night, when her pa came home from the mine, she asked him, "What was it like in the mine today, Pa?"

"Dark, my honeybee," he said. "Dark and hot. And the coal went rumble-rumble-rumble."

Belinda looked at the coal burning red in the fire. She thought about how it would be if it had a loud voice and rumbled.

Her pa took her on his knee, and he sang.

"Hush, my honeybee, don't say a word,
Pappa's going to buy you a mocking bird;
And if that mocking bird won't sing
Pappa's going to buy you a diamond ring."

Off went Belinda to bed in her little room that looked out, away, away, over the grassy valley to the other mountain. And she went to sleep.

She dreamed that her pappa gave her a silver ring with a big shiny diamond on it, glossy as a cherry. But the ring didn't fit – she could hardly squeeze it on her littlest finger. She tried and tried, pushed and pushed, but it wouldn't go on. Then, while she stood holding the ring between finger and thumb, the mocking bird came sailing across the valley on his grey and white wings, and gently took the ring from her in his beak. Away he flew again, over the brook at the bottom and up the other side. And there sat the boy on his rock – too far off for Belinda to see his face.

The mocking bird carried the ring to him, and he slid it on to his finger.

"Oh!" cried Belinda in a rage. "That's not fair!"

That woke her up – and she found it was morning.

In the evening, when her pa came home from work, she asked him, "What was it like in the mine today, Pappa?"

"Dark, my honeybee," her pappa said, ruffling her hair. "And hot. And the wheels whirred. And the coal crashed and scrunched."

Belinda looked at the red coal in the fire, and wondered what it would sound like if it began to crash and scrunch.

Then her pa took her on his knee, and he sang:

"Hush, my honeybee, don't say a word,
Pappa's going to buy you a mocking bird.
And if that mocking bird won't sing
Pappa's going to buy you a diamond ring.
And if that diamond ring's too small
Pappa's going to buy you a sky-blue ball."

Off went Belinda to bed, in her little room high up over the valley. The window was full of stars tonight. She lay awake looking at the stars for all of three minutes before she went to sleep.

She dreamed that her pappa gave her a beautiful blue ball, covered with golden stars. She tossed it and she caught it, she rolled it and she

48

bounced it, she threw it high in the air and then it came swooping back into her cupped hands. But after she had tossed and caught it a dozen times, the sky-blue ball suddenly slipped out of her clasped hands, and began to roll away down the hill. Faster and faster it rolled – until it looked like a blue streak with golden lines along its sides.

Over the bridge at the bottom it bounced – and the boy on the far hillside jumped up from his rock, and ran down and caught it.

Then he waved, and called something to Belinda, but what he called she could not hear.

"You give me back my ball!" shouted Belinda, so loudly that she woke herself up, and it was morning.

When her pa came home from work that night she asked him, "What was it like down there today, Pappa?"

"Dark and hot and dirty, my honeybee. Dark and hot and noisy. But never mind: tomorrow's Saturday, and Mama's coming home with a surprise for us."

And he took Belinda on his knee and sang:

"Hush, my honeybee, don't say a word,
Pappa's going to buy you a mocking bird.
And if that mocking bird won't sing,
Pappa's going to buy you a diamond ring.
And if that diamond ring's too small
Pappa's going to buy you a sky-blue ball.
And if that ball should chance to flee
You're still Pappa's little honeybee!"

Then he hugged Belinda and she went off to bed in her little high-up room that looked out over the valley. And, in a corner of the room, there was a new small bed that had not been there before. Belinda looked at it and wondered about it for all of two minutes before she went off to sleep.

And that night, in her dream, the boy across the valley threw back the sky-blue ball, and it came bounding and bouncing up the hill and settled in her hands. He sent back the mocking bird carrying the ring. Belinda put the ring on her finger, and it slid right on. And the mocking bird sang and sang, all night, most beautifully.

"Why don't you come too?" Belinda called to the boy. "Across the valley, to hear the bird sing?"

But he shook his head.

"What's your name?" she called.

"My name's Tom!" he called faintly across the wide distance of the valley. And he added something else that Belinda could not quite hear.

50

Next day Belinda's pappa stayed at home because it was Saturday. And he helped Belinda and her granny get the house all clean and polished and shining, with primroses and violets from the garden in every empty jam-pot.

And that afternoon Belinda's mother came home from the hospital with a new baby.

"There!" said Belinda's granny. "He's a lovely boy! He'll be a playmate for you, by and by."

"What's his name?" asked Belinda.

"We thought you'd like to choose it," said her mother. "He isn't named yet."

Belinda thought for a long time. Then she said, "Could his name be Tom?"

Bye,
Baby Bunting

Once there was a family called Bunting: father, mother, granny, brother, sister, and the littlest one of all, whose name was Hob. Father worked on the railways, Mother was a dentist, Brother was a huntsman, Sister had a job at a petrol station, and Granny stayed at home to look after Hob.

So, after lunch, when Hob had his nap, Granny used to sing:

"Bye, Baby Bunting,
Father's gone a-shunting,
Brother's gone a-hunting,
Mother's gone a-drilling,
Sister's gone a-filling,
All to get a splendid rug
To keep our Baby Bunting snug."

It was true that the blanket which covered little Hob's cot was rather old and worn and faded; it had been used for his elder brother, Tim, and his elder sister, Anna, before he was born; but he liked it all the better for that. It was old and pink and comfortable; it had a homely, woolly, friendly smell. He liked to curl up and drift off to sleep rubbing it against his cheek.

While Hob was awake, and while she was

doing things about the house, Granny used to tell him wonderful stories.

"Once upon a time," she'd begin, as she rolled out the pastry, "there was a giant. And he had a beehive, with bees as big as rabbits. And their honey was put into a pot as big as a bath."

"Yes, Granny," Hob would say. "And then what happened?"

"Then a princess came and stole the giant's honey."

"And then, Granny?"

"Then the giant was very angry!"

"And then? And then?"

Hob was happy to listen all day to his granny's stories.

In the evening the rest of the family came home, and they often brought things for little Hob. His sister brought him bunches of the wild flowers that grew beside the garage where she worked; and his father brought him little books of old train timetables, to chalk pictures in; and his mother brought tiny empty pots and boxes for him to keep his chalks and other treasures in.

But one day his brother Tim brought home a present that started off a lot of trouble.

It was a peacock skin.

"I shot it in the woods," said Tim. "Saw something flash and thought it was a blue jay. Blue jays do a lot of harm. But it was this peacock. Must have escaped from somewhere."

The peacock skin was stunningly beautiful. At one end there were bluey-green feathers that changed and shone as you looked at them, going from grass colour to black in the twink of an eye; while, at the other end, was the tail – a whole fan of feathers longer than your arm, dark and spider-webby, every feather with its own eye at the tip.

And what an eye! Each had a round centre, big as a plum, of dark, darkest blue. The blue plum had a nibble out of it on one side, and a ring of bright, brilliant green circled all round it and running into the nibble. Then, outside that, another ring of lighter, yellow-green.

And all those eyes seemed to be staring at little Hob.

Hob knew that the peacock skin rug was very beautiful – but it scared him.

The first night that it was spread on his bed, he never slept a wink; just stayed awake the whole night long, because he couldn't stop thinking about those eyes, all glaring into the dark.

Next morning, after all the family had gone off to work, to their shunting and hunting, to their drilling and filling, who should come to the house but a little old man all dressed in grey – grey suede shoes, grey leggings, grey breeches, grey tweed jacket, and an ermine cloak over the top – and he was in a towering rage.

"Do you know who I am?" he demanded.

"No," said Granny, who was clearing the

breakfast table.

Little Hob, still eating his porridge, sat with the spoon raised half-way and his mouth open, as the little man stamped about the kitchen.

"I am Lord Fossil! And somebody in this house shot my peacock!" the little man roared at Granny Bunting.

"Oh, my!" she said. "Oh, my dear, yes. That was my grandson Timothy. He *is* such a hasty boy. He *will* act before he thinks. He didn't mean any harm, I'm sure. He was ever so sorry as soon as he saw that it wasn't a blue jay. He made it into a bed cover for our youngest."

She pointed to Hob's little bed, with the peacock cover on it, all blue and green and eyes.

"Tim would tell you how sorry he was if he were at home, I'm sure he would," Granny Bunting said.

"Being *sorry* is no use! Being sorry won't bring back my peacock!" growled Lord Fossil. "Now I have only eight peacocks, and there ought to be nine. I shall put a doom on your house. The doors won't shut and the windows won't open, the kettle won't boil and the bread won't rise, the wind won't blow and the seed won't grow, the glue won't fix and the cake won't mix, until you put my peacock back together and he comes home to Fossil Park. And – last and worst of all – your baby there won't sleep a wink. Not a wink will he sleep, until my peacock is alive and walking again."

With that the little grey man stamped out of the kitchen and kicked the door shut behind him. But it immediately flew open again.

"Oh mercy me!" wailed Granny Bunting. She ran out of the door after the little grey man, but he was already out of sight.

Young Hob dropped his porridge spoon back into the bowl, and burst into a howl of fright. The bowl broke, and porridge oozed across the kitchen table.

From that day on, everything began to happen just as Lord Fossil had said it would.

The doors wouldn't shut, and the windows wouldn't open, although Father Bunting and Timothy oiled them and planed them and waxed

them and rubbed them and sandpapered them. The kettle would never boil, even if it was left on the stove till all the water had dried away inside it. Bread and cake mixtures came out of the oven as flat as they went in, although Granny and Mother and Anna beat the batter and banged away at the dough until their arms ached. No seed put into the garden would come up, and any dish that got broken had to stay that way, for no glue would stick it back together again.

And – last and worst of all – little Hob Bunting never slept a wink. Night after night through, he lay wide awake, lively as a cricket, asking if it was time to get up, asking for somebody to tell him a story, asking to go to the bathroom, wanting somebody to play a game with him, calling for a drink of water, asking if it wasn't breakfast-time yet.

All the rest of the family were kept awake too. They were dead tired, and so was little Hob; he grew very thin, and had big black circles under his eyes.

Poor brother Tim, who had brought home the peacock skin, was as sorry as could be.

"I'll never, never shoot another peacock," he said. "It was a most unlucky thing to do, and I wish I'd never laid eyes on the bird."

All the family were miserable.

"This won't do," Granny said one day.

She took a tea-cosy she had embroidered herself – on one side of it there were three tulips, pink, red and yellow, and on the other side was a small dragon – she wrapped the tea-cosy in tissue paper and off she went to see her old school friend Mrs Apple, the Wise Woman, who lived in the wood. Granny Bunting took along little Hob, too, in his push-chair.

"That's a fine tea-cosy, thank you, Emily," said Mrs Apple, and she slipped the cosy on to her teapot at once. The three tulips bounced off the cosy and put themselves into a vase full of water, while the little dragon stretched himself out and spun round and round the teapot so fast that he kept it hot.

"Now, what can I do for you, Emily?" Mrs Apple asked her friend, when they had had a cup of tea and Hob had had a mug of milk and a biscuit.

"Lord Fossil has put a curse on us because Tim shot his peacock," said Granny Bunting. "The doors won't shut and the windows won't open, the kettle won't boil and the bread won't rise, the wind won't blow and the seed won't grow, and glue won't fix and cakes won't mix; and, worst of all, little Hob can't sleep a wink and hasn't for weeks past. And he keeps the rest of us awake too."

"Well, to be sure, that's a bad curse," said Mrs Apple. "That certainly is a bad curse."

She drank the last mouthful of her tea, turned the cup upside down, tapped it three times, turned it the right way up again, and studied the tea-leaves inside. Then she said:

"You must cut the sun's hair and wash the moon's face. That's what the tea-leaves say will put the old man's peacock back together again."

"Cut the sun's hair and wash the moon's face?" said Granny Bunting slowly. "How am I supposed to do that?"

"Don't ask me," said Mrs Apple. "I can only tell you what the tea-leaves tell *me.*"

Old Mrs Bunting went home very thoughtful, pushing little Hob in his push-chair through the wood.

"Tell me a story, Granny," he said. "Or sing me a song."

"I'll sing you a song," she said. And so she sang:

"Hushabye now, my honey,
Hushabye, baby, croon,
We're off to cut the hair of the sun
And wash the face of the moon."

"And then what, Granny?" asked little Hob.

"Hushabye now, my honey," she sang,
"Hushabye baby, croon,
The sheep are gone to the silver wood
And the cows are gone to the broom."

"And what next, Granny?" asked little Hob.

"Stretch your arm to the sky, honey," she sang,
"Stretch your arm to the sky,
The birds are singing, the bells are ringing,
The wild deer come galloping by."

When the rest of the family came home that evening from their shunting and hunting, from their drilling and filling, Granny Bunting told them what Mrs Apple had said.

"We have to cut the sun's hair and wash the moon's face. That's the only way to put Lord Fossil's peacock back together again."

"How in the wide world are we expected to do *that*?" said Father Bunting.

"It does sound difficult," said Mother Bunting. But then she thought, and said, "No – no, wait a minute –"

"Yes!" said Anna excitedly. "In Skythorpe –"

"Yes!" shouted Tim even louder. "In Skythorpe –"

Skythorpe was the name of the nearest town, where Father and Mother and Anna Bunting went to work.

"In Skythorpe there's Sun, the unisex barber, right next door to Moon the launderette –"

This was perfectly true. Kim Sun had his hairdressing shop next door to Sue Moon's washeteria.

"I'll go there tomorrow morning," said Granny Bunting.

So next day she took little Hob and his push-chair with her on the bus to Skythorpe. It was a snowy winter's day and the bus rolled along

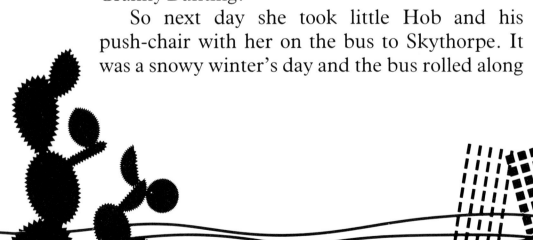

rather slowly. They didn't get there till after lunch-time. All the way, Granny told Hob stories – about the monkey's wedding, and the man who stole a haunted diamond out of somebody's pocket, and the town that got up and walked across the desert. All the passengers in the bus listened, and little Hob listened, sucking his thumb, for he was very tired, not having slept for weeks and weeks. If ever she stopped for a single minute, he asked, "And then what, Granny?"

When they got to Skythorpe they scrunched through the snow to Kim Sun's unisex hair salon and went inside. Kim Sun was leaning on the counter reading the paper, for on such a cold day there weren't any customers.

"What can I do for you?" he said.

"I need a pair of scissors to cut the sun's hair," said Granny Bunting.

"You want to cut my cousin's hair?" said Kim Sun. "You've come on the right day, and at the right time. See, out there, how long and lanky the sun's rays are shining."

Hob and Granny Bunting turned to look, and it was true: the sun was close to setting, and his

rays were shining in through the shop window, almost sideways on, level with the top of the counter.

Kim Sun rummaged about underneath his counter and brought out a pair of gold scissors, which he gave to Granny Bunting.

"What do I owe you for these?" she asked.

"Nothing at all. You can give them back to me afterwards. But you might bake me a simnel cake some time, in return for the loan, if you like."

"I'll be pleased to," said Granny Bunting, who baked very fine simnel cakes.

She and little Hob went out into the street, and they carefully cut the sun's hair.

"Thank you!" called the sun when they had finished. "That feels much more comfortable."

They swept up the sweepings with a brush and dustpan that Kim Sun lent them, and gave him back his scissors. Granny Bunting promised that, if all went well, she'd bring his cake in a day or two.

Then they went next door to the launderette, where Sue Moon was watching all her machines as they spun and whirled and squooshed and frothed.

"What can I do for you?" said Sue Moon.

"We need to wash the moon's face."

"No problem," said Sue Moon. "You've come at a good time. You can see her, right through the window. And it's true she could do with a clean-up."

66

Sure enough, there was the moon, big and silvery, staring through the shop window. But she had some dirty marks on her face.

"This will do the job," said Sue Moon, and she handed Granny Bunting a long-handled, extending sponge mop for washing windows. It was soaped all ready for use.

Granny and little Hob went back into the street, and she pulled out the handle of the sponge mop – out and out and out and out – until it reached right up to the silvery moon, and she was able to give the moon's face a good thorough wipe.

She did it three times over, for luck.

"Thank you!" called the moon. "That feels much better now."

"It *looks* better, too," said Granny Bunting.

Then they took the mop back into the launderette.

"What do we owe you for the use of the mop?"

"Not a thing! But you could bake me a Twelfth Cake, next time it's Twelfth Night."

"I'll do that," said Granny Bunting, who baked particularly good Twelfth Cakes.

Then she and little Hob rode slowly home on the bus. And all the way the sun and the moon shone extra bright, one on the left-hand side, one on the right. And all the way, Granny Bunting told Hob stories.

When they got home and opened the front door, out rushed a peacock, flashing like a handful of sparklers. It zipped through the garden and flew off down the road, with its tail trailing behind.

"Well, thank goodness for *that*," said Granny Bunting.

She put on a kettle for tea.

And it boiled in a twinkling. The doors shut

properly and stayed shut, the windows opened, the wind blew, and the seeds began to grow, Granny mixed a beautiful cake and put it in the oven, where it began to rise like a golden cloud, and best of all, while Granny was in the middle of telling little Hob a story about a magic fish, he yawned, and his eyelids started to droop.

"And *then* what, Granny?" he said.

Then he fell fast asleep, and Granny put him into his bed.

"Don't wake him!" she warned, when Father and Mother and Brother and Sister came home. "Whatever you do, don't wake him!"

But she need not have bothered. Little Hob slept snug as a dormouse under his old, comfortable pink blanket; and he didn't wake up till the middle of next week.

Oh, Can Ye Sew Cushions?

here's a very old house in the village of Dane Ambagh, where a family lived not long ago – mother and father, and five children. The father spent all week in the city, and only came home at weekends. The family were very rich. They had two cars, a swimming pool, three TV sets, four horses, and a billiard table – everything they wanted. Or so you would think.

There was one thing about their house that they didn't know. Every year, on a special day in winter, when the sun shone upon one particular spot on the floor in one particular room – if somebody – just at that moment – happened to be singing a special note of a special song – then, something might happen.

Mostly, of course, on that day, at that time, nobody was singing – and then nothing happened. The moment went by, was gone, the house had to wait for another year.

One snowy day in winter, all five of the children were sick with bad colds, and four of them were in bed. They had sore throats and runny noses, they were sneezing and coughing. The doctor wasn't able to come, because the road was all drifted over with snow. The girl who came daily to clean couldn't get there. The housekeeper said she couldn't stand it, she was leaving; and she left, then and there, with the farmer who brought their milk, on his tractor. He said he would take her to the nearest station.

So the mother and five children were left alone in the house, with the snow coming down.

What were the children's names? France, Jemima, Gervas, Toby and Sue. And their mother was Mrs Allways.

Mrs Allways had the same cold as the children. She was in the kitchen, stumbling about, trying to make porridge. She didn't know how, she had never done it before. Her throat was as sore as fire and her head ached badly.

Upstairs, France, the eldest girl, had pushed two big beds together in the playroom, and piled all the other children in them together, and heaped quilts and sheepskins and feather bolsters and blankets and hot water bottles around them.

She had a guitar, and she was singing her brothers and sisters all the songs she could remember, in a faint, hoarse, croaky, creaky voice.

"To a castle there came riding a knight," she sang,
"Riding on his little horse so white,
At the castle gate he stopped and stood,
'Now, tell me, are your children bad or good?'

"The lady looked down from the castle wall,
Down at the knight on his horse so small,
She said, 'Kind sir, it's very very sad,
But the children here are very, very bad.' "

As soon as France finished one song, the children, snuggled together under all the quilts and rugs, began to croak and whisper and beg. "Sing another song, Francey! Do, do sing another!"

So France thought for a minute, and plucked on her guitar, and sang again:

"When I was a young man, to my flock I did cry,
They weren't very many, they weren't very spry.
Sing hey! Sing hi! They weren't very many
Sing hey! Sing hi! They weren't very spry..."

"Sing another song, Francey! Sing another song!" So France thought for a minute, and

plucked her guitar, and sang again:

"I bought me a cat, and my cat pleased me,
I fed my cat under yonder tree,
My cat said Fiddle-I-dee.

"I bought me a hen, my hen pleased me,
I fed my hen under yonder tree,
My hen said shibby-shack, shibby-shack,
My cat said Fiddle-I-dee.

"Bought me a pig, my pig pleased me,
I fed my pig under yonder tree,
My pig said grapey-grapey,
My hen said shibby-shack, shibby-shack,
My cat said Fiddle-I-dee.

"Bought me a wife, my wife pleased me,
I fed my wife under yonder tree,
My wife said my honey, my honey,

Cow said ball, ball, pig said grapey-grapey,
Hen said shibby-shack, shibby-shack,
And my cat said Fiddle-I-dee."

"Sing another song, Francey! Sing another!"
"I can't think of any more," said France. "And I'm getting hoarser and hoarser. And I ought to go and help Mother. And, look, the sun's coming out, just a little."

Sure enough, there was the sun, like a pale silver penny shining down on the snow. For miles on miles, through the window, you could see moors and mountains, all covered in snow. And, close to the house, the sea loch, with dark water lapping along the rocky shore, and gold-brown kelp weed washing to and fro, to and fro.
"Do sing another song, Francey!"
"Oh dear," said France. "What in the world

77

can I sing? I really ought to go and see how Mother's getting on."

But she plucked at her guitar and sang one more song.

"Oh, can ye sew cushions, and can ye sew sheets?
And can ye sing balu-low, when the bairn greets?

"Hie-oh, ee-oh, what will I do wi' ye?
Black's the life that I lead wi' ye —
Mony o' ye, little for to gie ye,
Hie-oh, ee-oh, what —
oh what —
oh what
WILL I DO WI' YE?"

The house held
its breath.
Singing had made
France cough;
she coughed
and she coughed,
and wiped
her streaming eyes.

78

When she looked again, there was a woman in a shawl, standing in the doorway.

"Eh!" said the woman. "Eh, but I can see fine that ye need me sorely."

And with that she set to tidying up the beds and plumping the bolsters and making the younger children comfortable – they, all the while, looking at her with great eyes and mouths agape, like young starlings.

"Who – who are *you?*" stammered France. "Did – did Mother manage to get another housekeeper?"

"Nay, my young Mistress, your poor mither is in a swoon, flat on the pantry floor, and it's I must set to work and make breakfast for the lot of ye."

With that the woman walked quietly out of the playroom – so quietly that even a feather, which had drifted away from one of the bolsters, never stirred as her grey skirts swept past it.

"Who was she, who *was* she?" cried Jemima, Gervas, Toby and Sue.

"I don't know who she was," said France, much puzzled. "But I'd better go and help her."

Downstairs she ran, in her slippers and dressing gown, and found her mother laid out on the drawing room sofa, with a warm rug over her, fast asleep. And in the kitchen was the strange woman in the grey dress, stirring away at a pot of porridge on the stove. She had thick, long, white hair, that hung shining down her back, past her waist; it swayed to and fro as she stood stirring.

"Ach, my young Mistress, it's in bed you should be yourself," said the woman, "but since you *are* here, you can help me carry up these bowls. I have made the milk porridge, for that will be better for the young ones, and I have given your mother a fine posset with wine and honey and spices, that sent her into a deep sleep, from which she will wake mended and well."

"But who are you?" said France, taking the bowls.

"You will not have heard of my name. I was a proud princess once, but those days are long gone by. Pride was my undoing. And now I must wait to help those who need me; and long, long is the waiting, sore, sore is the grieving, before they will call for me."

"What is your name?" asked France, following, carrying the porridge bowls upstairs.

"You may call me Kirstan, young Mistress."

"Kirstie," said France. "We'll call you Kirstie."

All that long snowy day Kirstan looked after the children. She cooked for them, told them tales, played games with them, and took care of their mother too.

France noticed that, as evening came on, Kirstan began to look bideful and serious, as she sat skilfully mending one of Toby's little grey socks.

"What is it, Kirstie?" said France. "What worries you?"

"Children, there's a thing I must tell ye," said Kirstan, weaving the bright needle with its trail of wool swiftly back and forth across the hole in the sock which she held over her hand. "You called me in to help you, and glad I was to be here."

"Oh, and so were *we*!" said they all. "But how did we call you, Kirstie?"

"Ah," she said, "that I am not allowed to tell you. You must find out for yourselves. There is one way, and one way only, that you can be sure of bringing me, whenever you wish for me. But," she said again, "you must find out for yourselves."

"But what is the thing you have to tell us, Kirstie?" asked France, watching the silvery needle as it darted nimbly to and fro across the cobweb of dark grey wool.

"When you called me to help you," said Kirstan, "you opened the door to somebody else as well."

"Who? Who?" asked all the children.

"The Gribbin."

"Who is the Gribbin?" said France – still watching the silver needle as it sped to and fro across the web of wool.

"He is a kelpie. And, being a kelpie, he comes at night."

France knew about kelpies, but the younger ones did not.

"What is a kelpie? Tell us, tell us!"

"He is a wicked sea-beast from the old times. Bigger than a horse, he is, fiercer than a lion, with a horned head like a cow. And terrible teeth on him. And webbed feet. And wings on him. And he comes out at night only, and then he eats people. By day he cannot come. His name is the Gribbin."

"Oh, Kirstie! Where does he live?"

"Down in the sea loch yonder."

"And you mean he's going to come *here*?"

All the children trembled and huddled together in the middle of the bed.

France tiptoed over to the window and looked out at the loch, so black, in the dusk, its waves tossing up great bundles of gold-brown kelp along the snowy rocks at the water's edge. The light was going fast. It would not be long, now, till dark.

"Yes, the kelpie will come here," said Kirstan, busily mending away at Toby's sock. "But he cannot hurt you, not so long as you are asleep."

"But how can we be sure of *that*?" France asked, and she watched the bright needle weaving in and out, in and out, through the web of grey wool.

"How can we go to sleep, Kirstie? We shall be too frightened to shut our eyes!"

"You will sleep," she said. "Have no fear. Because I will sing you a special song. And when you listen you cannot help falling asleep. And then you will be safe, till morning, safe as if you were

locked up in a golden box – let the Gribbin rage
round the house how he will. So now, will you
have that song, or another story?"

At this, the children began to argue. The little
ones wished Kirstan to sing the magic song at
once, so they would be sure to be safe asleep
before the kelpie came. The older ones wanted her
to tell them just one more story – in case,

when they woke in the morning, she was gone, and they never found the way to call her back.

"Well, I will tell one more story," said Kirstan, looking out of the window at the sky. "It will not be full dark until the minute hand has crept up to five o'clock and the cuckoo comes out to tell us."

So she told them the story of a royal nixie girl, whose golden hair was so long and so strong that shipwrecked sailors wove ropes from it and mended their ship; that a lad, with one single hair, made a noose that caught a wild pony that carried him to fame and victory in the wars; and how the King of Norroway, with one golden hair knotted round his finger, was able to call the nixie maiden to him whenever he needed her help.

"And did she help the king, Kirstie? What did she do?"

But at that moment the cuckoo shot out of the clock and called five times.

"Hush!" said Kirstan. And she took Toby's

84

mended sock off her hand, put it with its fellow, and began to sing.

"Oh, can ye mend linen, and can ye darn shirts?
And can ye soothe troubles, and can ye heal hurts?
And can ye help sorrow, and can ye pay debts?
And can ye sing balu-low, when the bairn frets?

"Hie-oh, ee-oh, what will I do wi' ye?
Black's the life that I lead wi' ye –
Money o' ye, little for to gie ye,
Hie-oh, ee-oh, what
Will I do wi' ye?"

Before she had finished the first verse, all the children were fast, fast asleep, like a brood of starlings cuddled together higgledy-piggledy in the nest; France lay among them – but she held Toby's mended sock tight clasped in her hand.

All night long the black kelpie raged around outside the house, flapping his great wings, gnashing his great teeth, grinding his jaws together, scraping with his webbed claws at the windows and doors, leaving great gashes on wood and stonework. But he could not get in. And at the morning time he had to go back to his dark pot-lair, under the water of the sea loch.

All night the children slept, and they dreamed wonderful dreams.

In the morning when they woke, they were mended and better of their coughs and colds, quite better; and so was their mother. And not a one of them remembered anything – not a single thing – about the day before.

None of them, that is, except France. For she had watched and seen how Kirstan – whether on purpose or by mistake – had woven one of her own long, long shining white hairs in among the wool as she mended Toby's little grey sock. And in the morning, there it still was, woven into the sock that France had held in her hand all night long...

Lullay, Lulla

There was an advertisement that appeared every day for months in the pages of *The Times* – and many other papers as well, the *Surrey Journal* and the *Wessex Clarion*, the *Southern Advertiser* and the *Kent Echo* and the *Hampshire Courier*.

What the advertisement said was:

Will the person who advised us how to put our baby to sleep please, please come back and tell us how to wake him up again. Reward £10,000.

Tod and Dilly Dumbly, The Larkspurs, Camshott, Hants.

Well – as you might guess – Mr and Mrs Dumbly had a whole lot of answers to their advertisement when it first started appearing.

People wrote and telephoned, they came in cars and on motorbikes and horses, in taxis and Land Rovers and minibuses, by train, helicopter, coach and caravan. They had every possible plan for waking Baby Dumbly: rattles, rockets, revved-up engines, cannons, trumpets, trench mortars, amplified noises, soft noises, hypnotism, ultra-sonic treatment, z-rays, y-rays, even x-rays; not to mention touch-therapy, auto-suggestion, sunlight, moonlight, yeast injections and acupuncture.

Some of these treatments took ever such a long time, some of them were over in a second. Some of them the frantic parents allowed, some they didn't. (One idea that they didn't allow was running Baby Dumbly up into the air on the tail of a kite; another was sinking him under water in a plastic bubble.)

None of the treatments worked. Baby Dumbly slept peacefully on – sometimes smiling, sometimes chuckling in his sleep, as if his dreams just then were particularly funny and pleasing.

A local TV station took up the matter, then a national one. Baby Dumbly appeared on everybody's screen, smiling away in his sleep.

"Ah, the duck," people said. "If *I* were his parents, I wouldn't want to wake him up, the cherub. Why not
leave him
just as he is,

so peaceful, the angel? He's growing, isn't he, bless him, the little love, why should they worry?"

This was true. Fed in his sleep, Baby Dumbly seemed to thrive as well as any wide-awake child.

After a while, since none of the suggestions had worked, everybody lost interest again, even the doctors and the hospitals. They had more urgent ills to worry about. But poor Tod and Dilly Dumbly continued to fret and bother and grieve.

"It's all our fault the poor darling is the way he is," they said to each other. "We didn't take enough trouble over him. We must try and make up for it as best we can."

So they sat in turns by his cradle reading to him: Latin, Greek, Hebrew, books on history,

mathematics, geography, French, Italian, German, the Bible, Shakespeare.

"At least his education shan't be neglected," they said. "We *can* do our best about *that*, and we must, as we sent him to sleep in the first place."

What had happened was this:

One day in September, hot and quiet, Baby Dumbly was out in the garden in his pram, and, as usual, he was yelling his head off. He yelled all the time. He was bored. His parents were taking little notice of him. Tod was cutting the grass, Dilly was weeding the flower-beds; they didn't want to stop and take him for a walk. They were busy.

At about four o'clock, by rode an onion seller on his bike, strings of gold-brown onions dangling from his handlebars and packed in the basket over the back wheel.

"Need some onions, lady?" he said to Dilly, who was forking up buttercups among the lilies near the front gate. "Fine onions, four pounds a string, or ten pounds for three strings?"

"What I need," she said, straightening up, "is something to stop my baby crying and put him to sleep. I'd gladly pay ten pounds for *that*."

"Put your baby to sleep? No problem," said the onion man. "But have you any ear-plugs?"

"*Ear-plugs?*" says she, rather surprised. "Why yes, I do have a couple of pairs, as it happens. I use them at night sometimes because my husband snores so terribly."

"That's lucky. You'll need them," said the onion man. Then he fetched out a pencil and a tiny, grubby notebook from his jacket pocket. He wrote down a number. The number was so long that it covered two whole pages of the notebook.

Then he tore out the two pages and gave them to Mrs Dumbly.

"Now you must make me a promise," he said, shouting a bit above the baby's yells.

"Anything, anything!"

"As soon as you've done what I say, you burn those pages. If that number were to get known about the world, a lot of harm would come of it. Whole continents, whole races, whole generations would fall asleep. It wouldn't do."

"Yes, I'll burn the pages, *certainly* I'll burn them," says she. "But tell me quick – what do we have to do?"

By this time Tod, Mr Dumbly, had left his mowing and walked across the dry grass to find out what all the talk was about.

"This number," said the onion seller, "this number is a very, very ancient number; it goes back past Genesis and Exodus, many thousands of years; maybe back to the very start of things."

"What do we do with the number?"

"You dial it on your telephone. But first, make sure that you have the ear-plugs stuck firmly into your ears – or you'll fall asleep too. And, of course, the baby must be within earshot of the phone."

"Yes, yes, that's easy, the phone is on the front room windowsill, we can wheel the pram right outside the window," says Mrs Dumbly, all excited.

"My ten pounds," said the onion seller, politely.

Tod gave him the ten pounds and wheeled the pram right up outside the window, while Dilly flew upstairs and found the ear-plugs, and then each of the parents carefully blocked up their ears.

Meantime Baby Dumbly continued to yell his head off, and the onion man, whistling, got back on his bike and went on his way, who knows where?

Then Tod laid the two pages from the notebook, side by side, on the windowsill (luckily it was a very calm day, with no wind). He picked up the telephone receiver and began, slowly and carefully, to dial the enormously long number that the onion seller had written down. Just doing this took several minutes.

Now that he had the plugs in his ears, Tod couldn't hear whether his son was yelling or not; in fact Baby Dumbly, quite interested in these unusual goings-on, had stopped crying for the moment, and was watching his father through the open window. He saw Tod stop dialling, and reach his arm through the window so as to hold the telephone receiver close to the pram; then Baby

Dumbly heard a gentle voice out of long, long ago. It sang:

"Lullay, lulla, thou little tiny child,
Bye, bye, lullay, lulla.
Lullay, lulla, thou little tiny child,
Bye, bye, lullay, lulla."

It sang these words over and over and over again; would have gone on singing them as long as Mr Dumbly went on holding out the telephone receiver. But twice around was enough for his son, who sighed, yawned, stretched out his arms above his head, uncurled his fingers, curled them up again, and sank back on his mattress in a deep, deep sleep.

Mr and Mrs Dumbly, as they had promised, quickly took the two pages of notebook with the number written down, and dropped them into the garden bonfire, where they burned for two seconds and then crumbled away into white ash.

And, ever since that day, Baby Dumbly had slept...

Now it was September again. The garden looked very much the same as it had the year before. Mr Dumbly was cutting the grass. But his wife was sitting by the pram patiently reading aloud from a book of Latin poetry.

*"Qui nunc it per iter tenebricosum,"** she read sadly. Baby Dumbly slept on. A bicycle passed the

*"Now he is treading that dark road" – *Catullus*

front gate, then stopped, and a man called, "Need any onions, lady?"

Mrs Dumbly looked up from her book and let out a shriek.

"Why – why – it's *you!*" she squawked. "Tod – Tod – come quickly – look, look, it's the same man, it's the very same one who put our darling into this dreadful, dreadful sleep from which nobody has been able to wake him! Oh, please, please, tell us how to get him out of it, didn't you see our advertisement, we are nearly going distracted with misery and worry!"

The onion man tipped his beret sideways so that he could scratch his head.

"Put your baby to sleep, did I?" he said. "Why, that's right, so I did, it all comes back to me. But don't you want him asleep, then? You asked me to do it, didn't you?"

"Of course we did. But you didn't say that he'd never wake up again!"

"Oh, you want him awake now, is that it?"

"Of course we do!" cried Mr and Mrs Dumbly.

"Well, that'll come a *little* more expensive," said the man, rubbing thoughtfully behind his ear.

"Anything – anything!" cried Mr and Mrs Dumbly in trembling voices – though they did look sadly at their nice house and swimming pool and Rover car. Would they have to sell those?

"Twelve pounds, it'll cost, the waking up

process," said the onion man. "And don't forget the ear-plugs. Or you might suffer from aural shock."

With that he pulled out notebook and pencil, and wrote down a number. Even longer, this number was; it covered three whole pages, and he had to cram in the last four digits.

"There you are," he said, tearing out the pages, "that'll be twelve pounds, lady," – and Mr Dumbly gave him his twelve pounds. The man got on his bike and rode a short distance; then he put one foot on the ground and called back, "Don't forget to burn the pages afterwards."

Then he rode on his way, who knows where?

Mrs Dumbly had already hurried the pram to the window, her husband had raced upstairs for the ear-plugs, and as soon as they both stopped up their ears, Tod began, with a trembling hand, to dial the immensely long number.

It took nearly five minutes to do it; twice he went wrong and had to start again. At last it was done, and he held the receiver out of the window, beside his son's sleeping ear.

"*WAKE UP!*" barked a voice out of the telephone, and Baby Dumbly shot upright in his

pram. Tod joggled the receiver back on to its rest, and Dilly scurried off to poke the three pieces of paper into the heart of the garden bonfire.

They flew back to look at their baby. He was sitting up in his pram, totally wide awake. He looked back at them. Then he looked round the sunny, sleepy, empty garden.

Then he said, *"Sunt lacrimae rerum."*

"What did he say?" said Tod to Dilly.

"It's Virgil. It means, 'There are tears in everything,' " said Dilly.

"He talked in *Latin?*"

"Well, I've been reading Latin to him for a year," said Dilly – and then she picked her baby out of the pram and hugged him tightly, for he had begun to cry bitterly, as if his heart would break.

But Dilly carried him indoors, and gave him bread and butter and milk and apple sauce, and gradually, gradually, he began to smile a little, as he remembered all there had been to learn and laugh at and love and be amazed by, during his year of dreams.

Hushabye Baby
on the
Tree Top

There once was a man called Sam, and he had a wife called Minnie, and they had a baby girl called Carrie.

Carrie was as good as gold all day, but when the night came, and the wind began to beat against the windows, and bustle in the trees, and batter up and down the chimney, and bump against the door of the house, then Carrie would begin to cry. Why did she do it? Nobody knew. Nothing would stop her. She cried and cried and cried. She bawled. She howled.

"*I* don't know what to do," said Minnie.

"It's the wind as makes her cry," said Sam.

"Well, we can't stop the wind," said Minnie.

"And we can't stop Carrie," said Sam.

Sam had a job as a bellringer. Several times a day, sometimes at night too, he got on his bike, and rode off to the church, half a kilometre away, and went up the steps inside the church tower, and pulled the ropes that started the bells ringing:

"Ding dang dong bell, Dang ding dong bell
Dong ding dang bell, Ding dong dang bell."

Sometimes, when the wind carried the sound of the bells to the house, Carrie would stop her crying to listen.

"She likes the sound of the bells all right," said Sam when Minnie told him this.

One day, as Sam started off on his bicycle to ride to the church, the wind was so strong that it nearly blew his cap off. Sam grabbed the cap in his hand, just before it blew away down the road. And then – before he had time to put it back on his head – guess what fell into it! An egg, a crow's egg, which the wind had blown out of a nest, high up in the top of an ash tree.

Sam was astonished to see the egg in his cap. It was green, with brown patches.

Putting one leg on the ground, Sam let go of the handlebars and scratched his head with the hand that wasn't holding the cap. He wondered what he ought to do with the egg. For it must belong to somebody.

Just at that moment, two crows came flapping and fluttering down from the top of the ash tree.

"Oh, please, please, be careful with that egg!" called Mother Crow.

"It's our last one, do, pray take care! Don't drop it. It's our only child!"

"Oh, if it's yours, here you are," said Sam. "It seems quite all right, not cracked or anything. What a lucky chance that it fell into my cap."

"But how in the world are we going to get it

back into our high nest?" said Mother Crow. "It is too big for my beak, and if you carry it, husband, you are sure to crack it."

"You can hatch it in my garden greenhouse, if you like," said Sam. "There's a box of hay where it could lie. And you can fly in and out of the hole where one of the glass panes got broken."

"That's very kind!" cawed Father and Mother Crow. "We are very much obliged to you."

So Sam put the crow's egg in a box of straw in his warm greenhouse.

"What can we do for you in return?" asked Mother Crow, when she had inspected her egg to make sure that it was not broken, and listened to it, and settled it snugly into the rustly hay.

"If only you could stop my baby crying," said Sam. "Whenever the wind blows, she cries so hard that we are afraid she will do herself harm."

"Maybe she wants to be out in the wind," said Mother Crow. "Had you ever thought of that? Bring her out, and bring a net as well, and she can lie up in our warm nest."

So Carrie was brought out, tightly wrapped up, and settled in the net, and the two crows each took an end of the net in their beaks, and flew, with Carrie, to their big, bushy, twiggy nest at the very top of the ash tree. There they wedged her in. She fitted as neatly as a cork in a bottle. The nest was lined with hay and straw and feathers, and old, soft leaves; it was as warm and soft and bouncy as any bed. Up among the thin, whippy branches at the top of the tree, it swayed about most wonderfully whenever the wind blew.

Carrie loved being in the crows' nest. She was perfectly safe, because the crows hooked the net over her, on to the twigs; and from where she lay she could see nothing but sky – and the big round eyes of the two crows looking at her. She laughed with joy, waved her fists about, and grabbed the twigs that were within reach. When the wind blew, and the nest rocked, she laughed even louder.

"That was what she wanted," said Mother Crow. "She wanted to be out in the wind."

"But will she really be safe up there?" asked Minnie anxiously.

"Much safer than our egg was," Mother Crow said. "An egg will roll, but a baby can be fastened in. And a baby can hold on."

So, every windy evening, the crows carried Carrie up to their nest, and she spent the night with them, and she was so happy that she grew fast.

And, down below in Sam's warm greenhouse, the green and brown egg soon hatched. It broke

into three pieces and out stepped a black fluffy crow chick. From then on, Father and Mother Crow were kept busy all day long fetching him things to eat.

Crows grow much faster than human babies. In a few weeks Young Crow was able to fly out of the greenhouse with his father and mother, and visit Carrie, up in the nest at the top of the ash tree.

During the day, if it was fine and she lay in her pram in the garden, the Crow family would fly and flutter and flap round the pram, keeping an eye on Carrie, and telling her the news of what was happening in the world.

"Caw, caw! The baker's van is coming up the road. And Farmer Smith is ploughing his big field with a tractor – lots of worms are coming up! And Jennie Smith is going to the church to be married in her white dress."

"I know that," said Carrie. "Father has gone to ring the church bells."

And soon they heard the bells across Farmer Smith's field:

"Ding dang dong bell, Dang ding dong
Dong ding dang bell, Ding dong dang."

Sam rang the church bells for weddings and funerals, for morning and evening service, for holidays, Christmas and Easter and other special days; and it was also his job to ring the bells as a warning in case of trouble – if there was a flood, for instance, or foreign soldiers came riding into the country. But nothing of that kind had happened for years.

Young Crow and Carrie became fast friends. Young Crow brought her things to look at and play with – shining pebbles, and bottle tops, and daisies, and worms.

Soon Carrie was able to sit up in her pram. Then she wanted to learn to walk.

"Much better learn to fly," said Young Crow. "It is not at all difficult."

"I think I had better learn to walk first," said Carrie.

As Carrie grew bigger, her mother began to worry a little about her sleeping in the crows' nest on windy nights.

"She is getting so big and lively! Suppose she rolls out of the nest?"

"Oh, but we so love having her. Let her stay a little longer!" pleaded Mother Crow.

"Please let me go on sleeping in the crows' nest," said Carrie.

"Well – but only for a few more weeks," said Minnie.

One evening Sam and Minnie were

invited to a party at Sam's sister Brenda's house. Brenda lived in the town of Skythorpe, six kilometres away on the other side of the valley.

"No, no, we'd better not go," said Minnie. "It would be much too late for Carrie, if we took her with us. And we couldn't go to the party and leave her alone at home. Suppose burglars came? Suppose the house burned down?"

"Oh, nonsense," said Sam, who wanted to go to the party. "She won't be alone. We can leave her with Father and Mother Crow, and they will look after her. If burglars came, she'd be perfectly safe, up at the top of the ash tree. And if there was a fire, she would be better off, up there."

Minnie still felt anxious. But Sam wanted to go to the party very badly, so at last she agreed. Of course Carrie did not mind being left at all. She was perfectly happy, wrapped in her shawl and her net, up in the crows' nest, swaying about in the red and green light of sunset. The Crow family flew round her, cawing and bouncing in the wind – it was a windy evening, and growing windier still.

"Caw! Caw!" cried the Crow family. "Tuck yourself in well, little Carrie! There is rain coming behind the wind! We can see it far away over the hills, blowing this way like a great black bolster."

Soon, sure enough, the rain arrived. It lashed

and poured and pelted down, thick as macaroni, and the wild wind bounced the crows' nest up and down like a bouncing ball. Carrie didn't mind a bit; she laughed and laughed. She didn't get wet, for the Crow family perched around the edge of the nest and spread their glossy wings over her. The rain ran off their black shiny feathers, and Carrie kept quite dry and cosy.

But then, looking down, Father Crow said, "My gracious! There must have been a tremendous lot of rain farther up the river. Look how it is rising and flooding over the banks!"

Sure enough, the river was rising higher and higher. Soon it had flowed over the bridge. Then

the water came creeping up the road. Then it flowed over Sam's garden and into his greenhouse. Then the water was all around the house, up to the kitchen windowsill.

"My goodness!" said Mother Crow. "Sam and Minnie won't be able to get home tonight."

"We ought to warn them," said Father Crow.

"But how?" said Mother Crow.

"We ought to warn everybody," said Father Crow.

"But how?" said Mother Crow.

"I know!" said Carrie. "Go and ring the bells in the church! Fly through the window in the church tower and pull on the bellropes, the way that father does."

"Good! I'll do that," said Father Crow, who had often watched Sam through the window.

"And I'll help you," said Mother Crow.

"I'll stay here and keep an eye on Carrie," said Young Crow, and he spread his wings over Carrie as wide as they would stretch.

Father and Mother Crow flew away through the rainy, windy dark.

108

"Oh, I do hope they can get into the tower," said Carrie.

"Hark!" said Young Crow by and by. "They must have got in, for I can hear the bells."

Carrie poked her head out from under his wing and listened, as the nest swayed about in the wind. Sure enough, she could hear the sound of the bells as the wind blew in gusts:

"Ding dong – ding bell, Dang – ding dong – bell Dang – bell – ding dang, Dang – dang – dang – dang!"

The bells did not ring quite so smoothly as when Sam was pulling the ropes, but anyone could hear them, and anyone could tell that something was the matter. The bells rang and jangled and jangled and rang and rang:

"Thank goodness!" said Carrie. "Now Daddy and Mummy will know they can't get home."

She was very pleased that the crows had been so clever.

But then a frightening thing happened. The fork of the tree that Father and Mother Crow had built their nest in gave a great creak: WAAAAAAAAA – ERRRRRRRRRK! Then it gave another fearful creak and groan! WAA-AAAARRRRRK – RRRRRRNNNNNCH!

Then the whole top of the tree broke off – nest and all – and went whirling away on the wild wind. Carrie hung on to the side of the nest, and

Young Crow
spread his wings
and curled
his claws
and gripped
Carrie's net,
so that,
if she fell out,
he would still
have hold of her.
    But she
didn't fall out.
And the
nest stayed
firmly in
the crotch
of small
branches where
Father and
Mother Crow
had built it –
so cleverly
had they
stuck and
glued and
fastened it in,
with twigs
and mud,
and moss
and feathers.

"My! This is *really* like flying!" said Carrie, as they bowled along over the flooded fields.

"It isn't as good as flying," said Young Crow. "And I hope it stops soon, or father and mother won't know where we have got to."

Luckily – quite soon – the tree top blew down, and caught against the side of Farmer Smith's haystack. The lower part of the tree-trunk was in the water, but the fork, with the nest, and Carrie in it, was quite safe and firm, jammed in a corner where a piece of the stack had been cut out.

"Caw! Caw! Where are you, where *are* you?" called Father and Mother Crow, as they came flying back from the church tower.

"Here we are, here we are, quite safe!" called Carrie and Young Crow.

All night long the wind blew and the rain pelted down. But Carrie was snug and sheltered against the haystack, with the waterproof feathers of the Crow family all around her.

When the rain stopped and the sun came up, Carrie sang:

"Carrie and Crow they sat in an ash,
Hey, derry down, derry dido!
And the wind went woo! and the rain went
*   splash!*
Caw, caw, Carrie and Crow,
Hey, derry down, derry dido!"

Then they saw lots of people in boats, rowing

over the flood water. And among them, wild with worry, were Sam and Minnie. For they could see their house, up to its roof in water. They could see the big ash tree, with its top broken off. But where was Carrie?

"It's all right, she's here, she's here!" called Father Crow, circling over the muddy water.

"Safe on the haystack!" called Mother Crow. "Here she is!"

What a happy meeting it was! Carrie's parents hugged her as if they would never let go, and the Crow family flew round and round overhead.

Sam and Minnie thanked them, over and over, for ringing the alarm.

"If it weren't for those bells, a lot of people would have tried to cross the bridge, and they would have been drowned," said Sam.

"We shall have to stay with Auntie Brenda till the water goes down," said Minnie. "My goodness, it was lucky that we left Carrie with the Crow family and not in our house!"

It was two weeks before the flood water went down. And then it was a much longer time before everything was properly dry. All the carpets and curtains and cushions had to be hung out in the sunshine; all the plates and pots and pans had to be washed, for they were full of mud.

There were hundreds of worms for the Crow family to eat, and fish, too, which had floated away from their river in the flood, and then were not able to find their way back.

Carrie learned to walk in the muddy garden, with the drying blankets flapping on the clothes-line and the crows pecking among the muddy cabbages.

"Why don't you fly, why don't you fly?" called Young Crow, wheeling and flapping overhead.

Carrie put up her arms and tried to fly, but she couldn't.

"I think it's no use unless you have wings," she said.

Instead she learned to dance, and her dancing was very like flying. She bounded about, as lightly as a bit of tissue paper in a breeze. All day long she and Young Crow played games together, chasing each other over the drying grass.

Sam and Minnie had a stone built into the church tower with words on it that said:

THE CROW FAMILY
SAVED MANY LIVES
BY RINGING THE BELLS
ON THE NIGHT OF THE
GREAT FLOOD

and they wanted to give Father Crow a silver medal to wear, but he said politely that it would hinder his flying, so he gave it to Carrie to keep for him.

She and the Crow family loved each other all their lives. And when she was an old, old lady, Carrie was still friendly with Young Crow's great-great-grandson. He used to sit on her shoulder every day when she went for a walk, and he brought his children to tea with her every Saturday.

Four Angels to My Bed

T here was once a boy called John, the youngest of four brothers. One day, when he was still very tiny, and had only just learned to walk, little John's mother said to his father, "Do take the baby out of the house for an hour, husband – I want to finish washing the sheets and beating the feather pillows, and he gets underfoot, and the hot water splashes him, and the feathers make him sneeze."

So John's father carried the little boy up the street to visit the shop of their neighbour, Walter, a carpenter who made beautiful beds and chests and tables and stools and cupboards.

Today Walter was busy finishing off a bed.

Little John gazed round the workshop, which was full of tools, and sawdust, and planks, and pots of boiling glue, and the good smell of wood. Then he began to listen to what the grown-ups were saying.

"Look at that job of work, neighbour!" said Walter proudly. "The king himself couldn't ask for a finer bed. It's as big as a market-square. And you could travel from here to Rome before you found better carving than I put on those bedposts."

Little John's father put him down on the floor. And he walked slowly round the great bed, sucking his thumb, gazing up at it in wonder. It was made out of walnut wood, dark gold as amber, which had been planed and papered and rubbed and polished until it shone like a candle flame. The bed itself was so big that, to little John who was very small, it did seem almost as big as a market-place. There was no mattress on it, but a dust-sheet had been thrown across to protect the bed-slats, and the dust-sheet seemed to stretch out like a snowy plain.

Then the bedposts! How splendid they were! They rose right up to the ceiling, and held the square frame which would support the tester, or bed-curtain.

When the curtains are hanging all round, thought little John, it will be like a whole secret room inside there.

The four posts were each carved in the likeness of a man, a tall man stretching up one of his hands to hold the tester. But the men's faces were turned downwards, towards the centre of the bed. They were smiling in a friendly way. They had huge feathery wings, folded neatly down their backs.

If I were lying in that bed, thought little John, they would be smiling at *me*. They would be saying to me: "See! Here we are! You needn't ever be afraid of the dark, because we are here to keep watch over you, all night long."

"Well? Do you like my bed, little John?" asked Walter the carpenter, patting John's flaxen head.

Little John nodded. "When I'm a man, I shall have a bed like that," he said.

The two neighbours smiled at each other over John's head.

"Has this one shown any sign of his future calling yet?" asked the carpenter, scooping up a handful of tangly wood-shavings and stuffing them into a sack. "Will he be like his older brothers?"

"No, he hasn't shown any sign yet," said John's father. "But I don't suppose there's much doubt about the matter. In our family, you know..."

The two neighbours laughed, and then John's father gave some instructions about a chest he wanted made for his eldest son, who was nine years older than John and would soon be going away from home.

Little John wandered slowly round the bed again, looking at each of the bedposts in turn, trying to decide which one he liked the best.

One of them had a thin, thoughtful face, one looked a little sad, one looked very clever, one was round-faced and jolly. One of them had a winged lion rubbing against his robe, one had a scroll and a pen in a satchel at his belt, one held a paint-brush, one had an eagle perched on his shoulder.

"Do you know who those men are?" Walter asked John.

"Of course he knows!" said John's father. "Don't you, John? They are the four evangelists, the angels who wrote the holy books – Matthew, Mark, and Luke, and John."

"And this is your special one, little John," said the carpenter, pointing to the angel who held the pen.

John was pleased at this, for the angel who held the pen was the one with the smiling face. He seemed to be listening, hard, and wide-eyed, to some sound that he could hear in the distance – to some very beautiful sound, very far away.

The carpenter took out his notebook and wrote down the details about the chest; then John's father picked up his small son again and carried him home. By now the sheets were washed and hung up to dry, the pillows were beaten, the feathers were swept up, and it was John's bedtime.

He ate his bread and milk, then his mother helped him undress and washed his face and hands; then he went slowly up the stairs to bed, thinking all the way.

The stairs were old and black and very steep, specially where they went round the corner; little John went up them carefully on all fours.

"Don't forget to say your prayers!" called his mother up the stairs.

"No, I won't forget..." he called back.

In the little room that John shared with two of his brothers it was icy cold. The window glistened with frost, and a hundred stars outside the glass sparkled as big as ox-eye daisies.

Little John didn't waste any time. He quickly said his prayers:

> *"Matthew-Mark-and-Luke-and-John*
> *Bless-the-bed-that-I-lie-on;*
> *Four-angels-to-my-bed*
> *Two-to-bottom-two-to-head*
> *Two-to-hear-me-when-I-pray*
> *Two-to-bear-my-soul-away*
> *If-I-die-before-I-wake*
> *I-pray-the-Lord-my-soul-to-take —"*

Then he sprang into bed
as quickly as he could
and burrowed under
the big soft
feather quilt.

The bed which he had to share with his elder brother Fred was not in the least like the one he had just seen in the carpenter's workshop. It was just a small plain bed, with four plain posts at the corners.

Little John huddled under the quilt, trying to fetch up the courage to poke his cold feet down into the cold depths of the bed.

He was still partly thinking about the wonderful great bed in the carpenter's shop, and also about what the two men had been saying, above his head, as he wandered round and round the bed.

"Has this one shown any sign of his calling yet?"

"Not yet…"

Calling, thought little John. What did Walter

mean? What is a *calling*?

When mother is calling, John, John! it is because she wants me to come and hold the wool for her to wind, or let out the cat, or put away my shoes, or eat my porridge. What else could a calling be?

He lay in bed puzzling about it, and his feet felt colder and colder, and it seemed more and more impossible to send them down into the freezing place at the bottom of the bed. He wished his brother Fred would come up to bed. But Fred was much older and wouldn't come for hours yet.

Calling, thought little John. Who is going to call me?

The moon slipped round the corner of the window, and shone across the bed. Suddenly the quilt looked white as snow, and it seemed to stretch away, farther and farther, like a huge snowy plain, going as far as the edge of the world. And the four plain bedposts stretched up higher and higher, like trees, like enormously tall men with wings, until they vanished right through the ceiling. But he could hear their four voices from high above, calling him.

"John! John!..."

"Yes, what? Yes – what is it?"

"Stretch out, John! Stretch your arms out, stretch your feet out. Stretch your voice out. Stretch your soul out, John!"

Then he heard the four of them begin to sing.

124

How they sang!
Although all four
were singing together,
John could
plainly make out
each of their
separate voices.
Matthew sang
very simply,
a plain tune,
but a very
beautiful one
that rose
and fell
and rippled
like a brook.
Mark seemed
to sing all on
the same note,
but what a note!
It went
thrilling through
the room
and through
and through
the walls
and through
little John
until he felt
that it

must wake up the whole world. Luke's voice wove a beautiful pattern, in and around Matthew's tune, over and under it, like an embroidery to decorate a plain curtain. John sang the same tune as Matthew, but he sang it upside down and back to front, ending where Matthew began, beginning where Matthew ended.

How did little John know whose voice was which?

Well, he did know.

He felt so amazingly happy, lying there, listening, that he could have floated right up through the ceiling. Without even thinking about it, he stretched out his arms, across the bed, and his feet, right down to the bottom.

And then, without in the least meaning to, he began to join in the song himself. He found a new part, a part of his own, to weave in among the terrific, glorious sounds that the four voices above him were making.

"John?" called a voice up the stairs. "Is that you, singing in bed?"

"Yes, Mother…"

"Well, hush! You are supposed to be going to sleep. Have you said your prayers?"

"Yes, Mother."

"Goodnight, then!"

"Goodnight, Mother!"

Downstairs, Frau Bach shook her head, smiling, and said to her husband, "Well,

Christoph, I reckon that one's going to turn out like all the rest!"

"Better, maybe," said her husband.

Upstairs, little John Sebastian stopped singing, and added another line to his prayer:

"If I die before I wake,
I pray the Lord my soul to take;
But if I live the whole night through,
THIS *is what I plan to do . . ."*